Miss Yonkers Goes
BONKERS

MIKE THALER
Pictures by JARED LEE

AN AVON **C** CAMELOT BOOK

For Richard Brenner
in celebration of him
and all he does!

MISS YONKERS GOES BONKERS is an original publication of Avon Books. work has never before appeared in book form.

AVON BOOKS
A division of
The Hearst Corporation
1350 Avenue of the Americas
New York, New York 10019

Copyright © 1994 by Mike Thaler
Illustrations copyright © 1994 by Jared D. Lee Studio, Inc.
Published by arrangement with the author
Library of Congress Catalog Card Number: 94-94085
ISBN: 0-380-77510-7
RL: 2-3

First Avon Camelot Printing: September 1994

CAMELOT TRADEMARK REG. U.S. PAT. OFF. AND IN OTHER COUNTRIES, MARCA REC TRADA, HECHO EN U.S.A.

Printed in the U.S.A.

CW 10 9 8 7 6 5 4 3 2 1

Our teacher, Miss Yonkers,
usually behaves herself.
But for some reason,
today was different.

I should have known something was wrong
when the kids on the school bus
were quiet, and Mr. Balinski, the driver,
used his feet to steer.

When we arrived at school, Mr. Dreeber, the principal, was wearing a giant chicken outfit.

And Miss Yonkers had on untied sneakers, a baseball cap, and a torn sweatshirt.

She ran around the room
dribbling a basketball.
But instead of cheering her on,
the kids asked her to sit down
and call roll.

Miss Yonkers did a somersault and slam-dunked the ball right into the wastebasket. Then she sat down and started turning tardy slips into spitballs. One hit Freddy Farkle on the forehead and stuck.

The kids asked her to please open
her math book and teach decimals.
She did open her math book,
but she put it on her head.

Then she crossed her eyes
and boomed a colossal BURP!

The kids took out their history books
and started reading.
She took out the big map
of the Civil War, folded it into a glider
and sailed it across the room.

hen she turned her cap around backwards,
egan humming
Girls Just Wanna Have Fun,"
nd soon she was dancing on her desk.

When she finally finished the song,
it was time for recess.
She was the first one out the door.

She swung on all the swings
and slid down all the slides.

Then she hung on the tetherball rope
like Tarzan,
and wouldn't do *anything* "Simon Said."

When the bell rang
she wanted to stay outside.
The kids had to drag her back
into the classroom.

Once she was inside, she wouldn't open her English book. She just unwrapped ten pieces of bubble gum, stuffed them all in her mouth,

and blew a giant bubble that she popped on Melvin Mednick. Then she stuck the whole wad under her desk.

When she went up to the blackboard,
it looked like we were finally going
to have a lesson.
But she started drawing cartoons
of all the kids,

and making scratching noises
with the chalk.

Luckily, the lunch bell rang.
But in the cafeteria
she grossed *everyone* out!
She started making bubbles in her milk
and flipping peas across the table.

Then she squirted ketchup
at Stanley Splatman
and tossed mashed potatoes
at Marsha Plotnick.
She wanted to start a FOOD FIGHT!

But the class just tucked their napkins
neatly under their chins
and finished their lunches.

As we filed quietly out of the cafeteria she was squirting pudding out her nose.

In the afternoon
she didn't act much better.
Maybe even WORSE!
In Music she tried to play
the wrong end of the tuba.

In Art she finger-painted on everything but the paper.

**In Phys Ed
she let the air out of all the balls,**

**and during kickball,
she kicked the gym teacher.**

When we begged her for homework
she just stood on her head,
wiggled her ears,
and said, "Watch TV."

That was the last straw.
We went and told the principal.
But when Mr. Dreeber
put his head in the door,
she hit him right on the beak
with the basketball.

Boy, what a day!
I hope Miss Yonkers can act better
tomorrow.